JABARI TRIES

For all the Jabaris, young and old, in name and in spirit –
some of whom I've been lucky enough to connect with personally.
And for my cousins, who will be practically
grown by the time they read this: first there was Dantae
and then, quickly after, Aedan.

First published 2020 by Walker Books Ltd, 87 Vauxhall Walk, London SE11 5HJ • © 2020 Gaia Cornwall • The right of Gaia Cornwall to be identified as author and illustrator of this work has been asserted by her in accordance with the Copyright, Designs and Patents Act 1988 • This book has been typeset in New Century Schoolbook • Printed in China • All rights reserved. No part of this book may be reproduced, transmitted or stored in an information retrieval system in any form or by any means, graphic, electronic or mechanical, including photocopying, taping and recording, without prior written permission from the publisher. • British Library Cataloguing in Publication Data: a catalogue record for this book is available from the British Library • ISBN 978-1-4063-9553-2 • www.walker.co.uk • 10 9 8 7 6 5 4 3 2 1

JABARI TRIES

Gaia Cornwall

WALKER BOOKS

AND SUBSIDIARIES

LONDON • BOSTON • SYDNEY • AUCKLAND

"I'm making a flying machine today!" Jabari told his dad.

"Wow," said his dad.

"Me!" said Nika.

"My machine will fly all the way across the garden!" said Jabari.
"It'll be easy – I don't need any help!"

Jabari built an excellent ramp.
He put his flying machine at the very top.

Whoosh! Around ...

up it went! And CRASH

His machine did not fly.
"Maybe it's too heavy," said Jabari.

"Me!" said Nika.

"Not now, Nika," said Jabari. "I am concentrating. I need something to make my machine go up."

He thought about how inventors have to use their creativity and how engineers and scientists work to solve problems.

Lewis Howard Latimer

Dr Flossie Wong-Staal

Roy Allela

Dr Shirley Ann Jackson

Jabari gathered up all his tools. He prepared his space.

He sketched and planned.

"I think the ramp has to be big," Jabari said. "Really big."

After a lot of building and stacking and hammering and sticking, Jabari was ready.

"You know, I bet Nika would love to help out," said his dad.

Jabari looked at Nika. "I don't need any help," he said.

"What if you thought of her more like a partner?" said his dad. "Lots of great inventors have had partners."

"Me!" said Nika.

"We'll try it out," said Jabari.

"Maybe we need more power, Nika," said Jabari.

The engineers measured and mixed.

"Me?" said Nika.

Jabari handed his partner a stirring tool.

Trickle ... pour.

Twist ... turn.

Bubble, pop, fizz...

POW!

BASH

"Nothing is working!"

Jabari's chest felt tight, and his neck felt like a sunburn.

He wanted to cry.

He took a tiny rest.

"Hey," said his dad, "I see you're really upset."

"I'm frustrated," said Jabari.

"It looks like a frustrating problem," said his dad. "When I'm frustrated, I gather up all my patience, take a deep breath, and blow away all the mixed feelings inside."

"And then you try again?" asked Jabari.

"And then I try again," said his dad.

Jabari gathered up all his patience. He closed his eyes and took a deep breath. He blew away all his muddy feelings. He felt his body calm down. He felt his brain starting to work better.

Nika squeezed his hand.

"Let's try again," said Jabari.

The partners thought and thought together.

"Me," said Nika.

"That's it, Nika!" said Jabari. "Maybe we need better wings!"

They cut and glued and shaped and tied.
Tinker, twist, snap, snip!

Nika found the launch spot. Jabari held the
flying machine up, pulled back, and...

Whoosh! Up ...

"Wheeeee!" said Nika.

"You did it!" said his dad.

"We did it!" said Jabari. "It went all the way across the garden! We're great engineers!"

"We!" said Nika.

"And guess what?"

"What?" said his dad.

"Rocket to Jupiter is next!"

"Me!" said Nika.